POPPY'S PARTY
A CENTUM BOOK 978-1-911461-96-8
Published in Great Britain by Centum Books Ltd.

This edition published 2018. 1 3 5 7 9 10 8 6 4 2

Centum Books Ltd, 20 Devon Square, Newton Abbot,
Devon, TQ12 2HR, UK.

www.centumbooksltd.co.uk I books@centumbooksltd.co.uk
CENTUM BOOKS Limited Reg.No. 07641486.

A CIP catalogue record for this book is available
from the British Library.

Printed in China.

DREAMWORKS
Trolls

POPPY'S PARTY

by Frank Berrios

illustrated by Fabio Laguna,
Gabriella Matta and Francesco Legramandi

4

This is Troll Village.
It is the happiest place
– with the happiest trees
and the happiest creatures.
They are called Trolls.
It is also the place
Poppy calls home!

Poppy loves
to dance and sing.
She also loves
to sing and dance.
And today she gets to do both!
She is very excited.

Poppy is going to throw
the biggest, loudest,
craziest party ever!
King Peppy can't wait!

Everyone is getting ready
for Poppy's party.
But first Poppy has to
hand out the invitations!

Poppy's friend Smidge

is super small but super strong.

She gives Poppy a super lift!

Poppy brings Biggie
an invitation.
He is a big softie.
He cries happy tears.

Poppy visits Creek.
He always gives good advice
and everyone hangs
on his every word.
Creek is a super-cool Troll.

Poppy knows that Guy Diamond

will make her party shine.

He shakes off a cloud

of glitter whenever he dances!

Poppy drops in to see the twins,
Satin and Chenille.

Poppy's fashionable friends
will create awesome dresses
for her to wear before, during
and after the party!

Poppy practises
her dance moves with Cooper.
No one can dance like Cooper.
That's because he is the only
Troll with four feet!

DJ Suki is creating a special playlist for Poppy's after-party. DJ Suki uses all sorts of critters to make music. She is always ready to drop the beat!

Poppy's friend Fuzzbert loves
to tickle the Trolls. He is also
a tickler on the dance floor!

Branch is a very different Troll.

He does not like to sing.

He does not like to dance.

He does not like to sing

or dance or hug!

Poppy gives Branch
a special invitation.
She knows she can help
him find his true colours.
With a song in your heart,
you can do anything!

At the party, Smidge sends
glitter sparkles into the sky.
DJ Suki turns up the volume.
She makes it loud!

The Trolls sing and dance,
and hug and sing
and dance and hug
at Poppy's biggest,
loudest, craziest
party ever!

Everything is rainbows
and cupcakes.
Hug Time!

READING TIPS

We hope you and your child enjoy reading this picture book.

Try to make time to read with your child every day and make reading together something you both look forward to.

A good way to bring a book to life is to put on different voices for different characters in the story.

You could also stop at certain points in the book to ask your child what they think about the characters, what is happening in the story and what they think might happen next.

You can still read aloud to your child, even when they are confident enough to read by themselves.

If your child is excited about the subject they are reading about, it will help them to retain their interest in reading.

A love of reading can last a lifetime!